W9-BIY-045

Henry and Mudge IN Puddle Trouble

The Second Book of Their Adventures

Story by Cynthia Rylant

Pictures by Suçie Stevenson

Ready-to-Read

Simon Spotlight
New York London Toronto Sydney

For the Halems: Sandy, Henry and Jess—CR

For Frank Modell—SS

THE HENRY AND MUDGE BOOKS

First Aladdin Paperbacks Edition, 1990

Simon Spotlight
An imprint of Simon & Schuster Children's Publishing Division
1230 Avenue of the Americas
New York, NY 10020

Also available in a Simon & Schuster Books for Young Readers Edition.

Printed and bound in the United States of America

40 39 38 37 36

The Library of Congress has cataloged the hardcover edition as follows:
Rylant, Cynthia.
Henry and Mudge in puddle trouble: the second book of their adventures / story by Cynthia Rylant; pictures by Suçie Stevenson.
p. cm.
Summary: For Henry and his big dog Mudge, spring means admiring the first snow glory, playing in puddles in the rain, and watching the five new kittens next door.
[1.Dogs—Fiction. 2. Spring—Fiction.] I.Stevenson, Suçie, ill. II. Title.
PZ7.R982Hkk 1990
[E]-dc20 89-39810 CIP AC
ISBN-10: 0-689-81002-4 (hc.)
ISBN-13: 978-0-689-81003-9 (Aladdin pbk.)
ISBN-10: 0-689-81003-2 (Aladdin pbk.)
0215 LAK

Contents

The Snow Glory 5

Puddle Trouble 21

The Kittens 37

The Snow Glory

When the snow melted
and Spring came,
Henry and his big dog Mudge
stayed outside
all the time.

Henry had missed
riding his bike.
Mudge had missed
chewing on sticks.
They were glad
it was warmer.

One day when Henry and Mudge
were in their yard,
Henry saw something blue
on the ground.
He got closer to it.
"Mudge!" he called.
"It's a flower!"
Mudge slowly walked over
and sniffed the blue flower.

Then he sneezed
all over Henry.
"Aw, Mudge," Henry said.

Later, Henry's mother
told him that the flower
was called a snow glory.
"Can I pick it?"
Henry asked.
"Oh, no," said his mother.
"Let it grow."
So Henry didn't pick it.

Every day he saw the snow glory
in the yard,
blue
and looking so pretty.
He knew he shouldn't pick it.
He was trying not to pick it.
But he thought how nice
it would look in a jar.
He thought how nice
to bring it inside.
He thought how nice
it would be
to own that snow glory.
Every day he stood with Mudge
and looked at the flower.

Mudge would stick his nose
into the grass
all around the snow glory.
But he never looked at it
the way Henry did.
"Don't you think the snow glory
has been growing long enough?"
Henry would ask his mother.
"Let it grow, Henry,"
she would say.

Oh, Henry wanted that snow glory.
And one day
he just knew
he had to have it.
So he took Mudge
by the collar
and he stood
beside the snow glory.

“I’m going to pick it,”
Henry whispered to Mudge.
“I’ve let it grow a long time.”
Henry bent his head and
he said in Mudge’s ear,
“Now I *need* it.”
And Mudge wagged his tail,
licked Henry’s face,
then put his big mouth
right over that snow glory . . .

and he ate it.

"*No, Mudge!*" Henry said.

But too late.

There was a blue flower

in Mudge's belly.

"I said *need* it, not *eat* it!"
shouted Henry.
He was so mad because
Mudge took his flower.
It was Henry's flower
and Mudge took it.

And Henry almost said,
"Bad dog," but he stopped.

He looked at Mudge,
who looked back at him
with soft brown eyes
and a flower in his belly.

Henry knew it wasn't his snow glory.

He knew it wasn't anybody's snow glory.

Just a thing to let grow.

And if someone ate it,

it was just a thing to let go.

Henry stopped feeling mad.

He put his arms around

Mudge's big head.

"Next time, Mudge,"
he said,
"try to *listen* better."
Mudge wagged his tail
and licked his lips.
One blue petal
fell from his mouth
into Henry's hand.
Henry smiled,
put it in his pocket,
and they went inside.

Puddle Trouble

In April
it rained
day after day
after day
after day.

Henry was getting bored.
Mudge was chewing up
everything in the house.
So Henry said,
"Let's play outside anyway."

He put on his raincoat
and sneakers
and went outside with Mudge.
Henry forgot to ask his father
if it was all right.

When Mudge stepped
into the wet grass,
he lifted his paws
and shook them.
"Too bad you don't
have sneakers," Henry said.
And he walked in a circle
around Mudge.
Squish, squish, squish, squish.

Mudge listened
and looked at Henry.
Then he got closer
to Henry
and wagged his tail
and shook the water from
his big wet furry body
all over Henry.
Henry wiped the water
from his face.
"Aw, Mudge," he said.

The two of them
went walking.
And down the road
they found a big puddle.
A giant puddle.
A lake puddle.
An ocean puddle.
And Henry said, "Wow!"

He started running.

Mudge got there first.

SPLASH!

Muddy water all over Mudge.

SPLASH!

Muddy water all over Henry.

It was the biggest,

deepest puddle

they had ever seen.

And they loved it.

When Henry's father
called for Henry
and didn't find him,
he went outside.
He looked down the road.
SPLASH! he heard.
He put on his raincoat
and went walking.

SPLASH! he saw.
Henry's father saw Mudge,
with a muddy face
and muddy tail
and muddy in between.

Henry's father saw Henry,
with a muddy face
and muddy sneakers
and muddy in between.
And he yelled, "*Henry!*"
No more splashes.
Just a boy and a dog,
dripping.
"Hi, Dad," Henry said,
with a little smile.
Mudge wagged his tail.
"Henry, you know
you should have asked me first,"
Henry's father said.
"I know," said Henry.

"I am surprised at you,"
Henry's father said.
"I'm sorry," said Henry.
"I don't know what to do
with you," Henry's father said.
Henry looked sad.
Then Mudge wagged his tail,
licked Henry's hand,
and shook the water
from his big wet furry body
all over Henry and Henry's father.

"*Mudge!*" Henry yelled.
Henry's father stood there
with a muddy face
and muddy shoes
and muddy in between.
He looked at Mudge,
he looked at Henry,
he looked at the big puddle.

Then he smiled.
"Wow," he said.
And he jumped in.

He splashed water on Mudge.

He splashed water on Henry.

He said, "Next time, ask me along!"

Henry said, "Sure, Dad."

And Henry splashed him back.

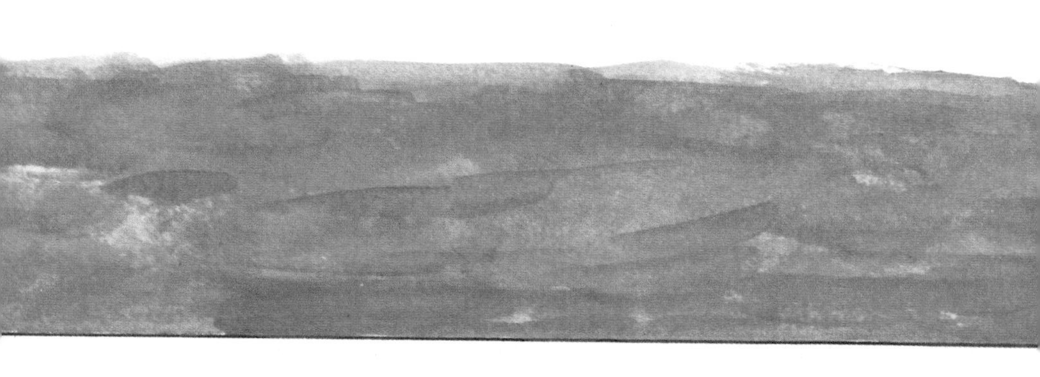

The Kittens

In May the cat who lived
next door to Henry and Mudge
had a litter of kittens.
There were five kittens.
One was orange.
One was gray.
One was black and white.
And two were all black.

The kittens sometimes stayed
in a box in their front yard
to get some sun
while the mother cat rested.
One day Henry and Mudge
peeked in the box.
They saw tiny little
kitten faces
and tiny little
kitten paws
and heard tiny little
kitten meows.

Mudge sniffed

and sniffed and sniffed.

He wagged his tail

and sneezed

and sniffed some more.

Then he put his

big head into the box

and with his big tongue

he licked

all five kittens.

Henry laughed.
"Do you want
some kittens of your own?"
he asked Mudge.
Mudge grunted
and wagged his tail again.
Whenever the kittens
were in their front yard,
Henry and Mudge
visited the box.
Henry loved their
little noses.
And he had even
given them names.

He called them
Venus,
Earth,
Mars,
Jupiter,
and Saturn.
Henry loved planets, too.

While Henry was at school one day,
a new dog came up Henry's street.
The five kittens
were sleeping
in the box in their yard.
Mudge was sleeping in Henry's house.

When the new dog
got closer to Henry's house,
Mudge's ears went up.

When the new dog
got even closer
to Henry's house,
Mudge's nose went in the air.
And just when the new dog
was in front of
Henry's house,
Mudge barked.

He barked and barked
and barked
until Henry's mother
opened the door.

And just as
Mudge ran out the door,
the new dog
was in the neighbor's yard,
looking in the kittens' box.
And just as the new dog
was putting his big teeth into the box,
Mudge ran up behind him.

SNAP! went Mudge's teeth
when the new dog saw him.
SNAP! went Mudge's teeth again
when the new dog looked back
at the box of kittens.

Mudge growled.

He looked into the eyes of the new dog.

He stood ready to jump.

And the new dog backed away

from the box.

He didn't want the kittens anymore.

He just wanted to leave.

And he did.

Mudge looked in the kitten box.
He saw five tiny faces
and five skinny tails
and twenty little paws.
He reached in and licked
all five kittens.

Then he lay down
beside the box
and waited for Henry.
Venus,
Earth,
Mars,
Jupiter,
and Saturn
went back to sleep.